# Caps
# for Sale

*A tale of a peddler, some monkeys, and
their monkey business*

Story and Pictures by

ESPHYR SLOBODKINA

**Scholastic Inc.**
New York Toronto London Auckland Sydney

ISBN 0-590-41080-6

24                                                    4 5 6 7/9

Printed in the U.S.A.                    23

*To Rosalind and Emmy Jean,*
*and to their grandfather*
*who loved to read to them*

Once there was a peddler who sold caps.
But he was not like an ordinary peddler,
carrying his wares on his back.
He carried them on top of his head.

First he had on his own checked cap,
    then a bunch of gray caps,
    then a bunch of brown caps,
    then a bunch of blue caps,
and, on the very top, a bunch of red caps.

He walked up and down the streets,
holding himself very straight
so as not to upset his caps.

As he went along he called,
"Caps! Caps for sale! Fifty cents a cap!"

One morning he couldn't sell any caps.
He walked up the street and he walked
down the street calling,
"Caps! Caps for sale. Fifty cents a cap."

But nobody wanted any caps that
morning. Nobody wanted even a red cap.

He began to feel very hungry,
but he had no money for lunch.

"I think I'll go for a walk in the country," said he.
And he walked out of town —
slowly, slowly, so as not to upset his caps.

He walked for a long time until he came to a great big tree.

"That's a nice place for a rest," thought he.

And he sat down very slowly
under the tree
and leaned back little by little
against the tree trunk,
so as not to disturb the caps on his head.

Then he put up his hand to feel if they
were straight —
        first his own checked cap,
        then the gray caps,
        then the brown caps,
        then the blue caps,
        then the red caps on the very top.

They were all there.

So he went to sleep.

He slept for a long time.

When he woke up, he was refreshed and rested.

But before standing up he felt with his hand
to make sure his caps were in the right place.

All he felt was his own checked cap!

He looked to the right of him.
No caps.

He looked to the left of him.
No caps.

He looked in back of him.
No caps.

He looked behind the tree.
No caps.

Then he looked up into the tree.

And what do you think he saw?

On every branch sat a monkey.

On every monkey

was a gray, or a brown, or a blue, or a red cap!

The peddler looked at the monkeys.

The monkeys looked at the peddler.

He didn't know what to do.

Finally he spoke to them.

"You monkeys, you," he said, shaking a finger at them, "you give me back my caps."

But the monkeys only shook their fingers back at him and said, "Tsz, tsz, tsz."

This made the peddler angry, so he shook
both hands at them and said,
"You monkeys, you!
You give me back my caps."

But the monkeys only shook their
hands back at him and said, "Tsz, tsz, tsz."

Now he felt quite angry.
He stamped his foot, and he said,
"You monkeys, you!
You better give me back my caps!"

But the monkeys only stamped their feet
back at him and said, "Tsz, tsz, tsz."

By this time the peddler was really very,
very angry.
He stamped both his feet and shouted,
"You monkeys, you!
You must give me back my caps!"

But the monkeys only stamped both their
feet back at him and said, "Tsz, tsz, tsz."

At last he became so angry
that he pulled off his own cap,
threw it on the ground,
and began to walk away.

But then each monkey pulled off his cap . . .

and all the gray caps,

and all the brown caps,

and all the blue caps,

and all the red caps
came flying down out of the tree.

So the peddler picked up his caps
and put them back on his head —

first his own checked cap,

then the gray caps,

then the brown caps,

then the blue caps,

then the red caps on the very top.

And slowly, slowly,
he walked back to town calling,
"Caps! Caps for sale! Fifty cents a cap!"

## About the Author

ESPHYR SLOBODKINA was born in
Cheliabinsk, Russia. She grew up in Siberia and
Manchuria and emigrated to the
United States in 1928. She attended the
National Academy of Design in New York City,
and her artwork is represented in various
museums and private collections. She is
best known, however, for her children's
books, which have a distinctive charm
rooted in both folklore and modern graphic
design. *Caps for Sale* is one of the most
popular books ever written for children
and has found its place on the all-time
best-seller list. Ms. Slobodkina is the
author/illustrator of more than fifteen
other books for children, and she has
illustrated several books by Margaret Wise
Brown, including *The Little Fireman,
The Little Cowboy,* and *Sleepy ABC*.